SANDWICH

SANDWICH

RECIPES: YISRAEL AHARONI
PHOTOGRAPHY: NELLI SHEFFER
DESIGN: EDDIE GOLDFINE
EDITOR: ANN KLEINBERG

1❍
TEN SPEED PRESS
Berkeley | Toronto

To Noa Daniel and Roni

Copyright © 2004 by Penn Publishing Ltd.
And Aleh Publishing
All rights reserved. No part of this book may be
reproduced in any form, except brief excerpts for
the purpose of review, without written permission of
the publisher.

Ten Speed Press
P.O. Box 7123
Berkeley, California 94707
www.tenspeed.com

Distributed in Australia by Simon & Schuster Australia,
in Canada by Ten Speed Press Canada, in New
Zealand by Southern Publishers Group, in South Africa
by Real Books, and in the United Kingdom and Europe
by Airlift Book Company.

Cover and book design by Eddie Goldfine
Photography by Nelli Sheffer
Editing by Ann Kleinberg

Library of Congress Cataloging-in-Publication Data
on file with the publisher.
1-58008-600-4

Printed in Hong Kong
First printing, 2004

1 2 3 4 5 6 7 8 9 10 — 09 08 07 06 05 04

Contents

Ah, the glorious SANDWICH. Is there any food more universally consumed?

From ancient times through modern, this combination of bread and filling has found its way into myriad cuisines. Who doesn't love a sandwich? It knows no age or cultural barriers and is accepted everywhere as a quick, NOURISHING MEAL. Can you think of a school lunch without PEANUT BUTTER and jelly? A break from work without a quickly gobbled BLT or steak-and-onion hero? The burrito? The falafel in a pita? The quintessential BURGER on a bun? From the moment the first genius combined two pieces of BREAD with a filling, no food has come close in popularity.

Legend has it that the origin is credited to JOHN MONTAGUE, the fourth Earl of Sandwich. As he was furiously gambling away his fortune in a London club back in 1762, he refused to leave the table to dine. He ordered all his food brought to him between two slices of bread, thereby enabling him to hold his MEAL in one hand while continuing to play. Fellow gamblers were inspired, ordered "the same as Sandwich", and culinary history was made.

The sandwich has never been as popular as it currently is. The CHOICES of bread alone are mind-boggling: whole wheat, SOURDOUGH, focaccia, pita, tortilla, bagel, and raisin-walnut, to name just a few. And the fillings? Endless varieties. From simple to SOPHISTICATED, one's sandwich options are limited only by the level of desire and creativity. It can serve as a complete meal—combining carbohydrate, protein, and vegetables—or as a delicious snack.

SANDWICH will delight its reader with a refreshingly new look at sandwiches. With a slightly Mediterranean flair, the emphasis is on hearty breads, VARIOUS MEATS and cheeses, fresh vegetables, and an assortment of SPREADS, oils, and herbs. Onions may be raw or grilled. Cheese may be sliced or melted. Even bananas, chocolate, and COGNAC are included among the ingredients. The message is that sandwich possibilities are infinite—it's just a matter of imagination and the contents of the nearest REFRIGERATOR.

The book is divided into five sections: Sandwiches takes a new look at old FAVORITES; Bruschetta honors that wonderful ITALIAN invention of grilled, crunchy bread with tasty toppings; Toasts includes a whole lot more than grilled cheese; SWEET Sandwiches is for those who love bread and sweets and YEARN for a marriage of both; and last but not least, there's Between the Bread, with recipes for fillings, spreads, tapenades, and FLAVORED OILS that are featured in the book.

Most RECIPES are for two sandwiches—but can be easily multiplied for more. The beautiful photographs will make your MOUTH water just looking at them—imagine how good they will be to taste. The cleverly designed format puts the BOOK squarely in the palm of your hand—just like a sandwich. You will begin to think of a sandwich not only as a SOURCE of nourishment but also as a basis for a whole NEW WORLD of creative adventures in the kitchen.

Enjoy reading *Sandwich* and when you are finished—go and make yourself one!

SANDWICHES

Ricotta,
Grilled Zucchini,
and Pine Nuts

2 small zucchini

1 tablespoon extra
virgin olive oil, plus
extra for drizzling

Salt

Freshly ground black
pepper

1 teaspoon fresh thyme
leaves

10 green olives, pitted

1 tablespoon pine nuts

2/3 cup ricotta cheese

4 slices dark rye bread

Cut the zucchini lengthwise into 1/2-inch-thick slices. Brush both sides with the olive oil. Sprinkle with salt, pepper, and the thyme. Place in a grill pan heated to a high temperature and cook for 2 minutes on each side, until the slices are slightly charred.

Cut the olives in half lengthwise. Toss for a few minutes in a dry skillet over medium heat and then combine with the pine nuts.

Spread the cheese onto 2 slices of the bread, drizzle with a little olive oil, and scatter the olives and pine nuts on top. Top with 2 to 3 slices of zucchini, cover with the remaining bread slices and serve.

Feta, Roasted Peppers, *and* Tapenade

2 fresh French rolls

5-ounce chunk of feta cheese

2 tablespoons tapenade (page 99)

4 roasted red pepper halves (page 98)

8 fresh basil leaves

Slice open the rolls. Cut the feta cheese into 4 slices. Spread 1 tablespoon of the tapenade on the bottom of each roll. Top with 2 slices of cheese, 2 roasted pepper halves, and 4 basil leaves. Cover with the other roll half and press down slightly.

Roast Beef *with* Balsamic Roasted Onions *and* Garlic

4 slices whole-wheat sourdough bread

Dijon mustard or garlic mayonnaise (page 103)

5 ounces roast beef

Coarse salt

Freshly ground black pepper

Mixed salad greens

1 tomato, sliced

3 balsamic roasted onions (page 101)

4 cloves balsamic roasted garlic (page 101)

Spread 2 slices of the bread with the mustard or mayonnaise. Divide the roast beef between the two slices and season with salt and pepper.

Top with the mixed greens, tomato slices, balsamic roasted onions, and garlic. Cover with the remaining bread slices.

North African Potato, Hard-Boiled Egg, *and* Chile Spread

2 pita pockets

2 cooked potatoes

2 hard-boiled eggs

Harissa (available in Middle Eastern markets) or chile spread (page 98)

Juice of 1 lemon

Cumin

Salt

Freshly ground black pepper

Olive oil, for garnish

Chopped cilantro leaves, for garnish

Slit open the edge of the pita pocket halfway around. Dice the potatoes and eggs and stuff them into each pocket, slightly mashing with a fork. Add a bit of the harissa, the lemon juice, and cumin, salt, and pepper to taste. Drizzle in a small amount of olive oil and sprinkle with the chopped cilantro leaves.

Focaccia *with* Zucchini *and* Mint Frittata

2 zucchini

3 tablespoons olive oil

2 cloves garlic, crushed

1 green chile pepper, seeded and finely chopped

2 tablespoons coarsely chopped mint

1/4 cup coarsely chopped parsley

2 scallions, thinly sliced

4 eggs

3 tablespoons grated Parmesan cheese

Salt

Freshly ground black pepper

2 (5-inch) squares focaccia (page 104)

Cut the zucchini into cubes. Heat the oil in a large skillet and add the garlic, chile pepper, and zucchini. Sauté until the garlic starts to turn golden. Keep stirring and add in the mint, parsley, and scallions.

Beat the eggs with the Parmesan, and season with salt and pepper. Pour into the skillet over the zucchini mixture and cook over medium heat for 5 to 7 minutes, until the bottom starts to turn brown. Carefully flip the frittata over onto a plate and slip it back into the pan. Cook the other side for 3 to 4 minutes. Remove from pan and set aside for about 30 minutes.

Cut each focaccia square on the diagonal and slice open. Cut the frittata into wedges and slip between the focaccia pieces. Press down so that the bread absorbs some of the oil.

Tuna, Red Onion,
and Olives

1 Mediterranean round bread (like a large pita pocket)

1 (6-ounce) can chunk light tuna in olive oil

2 tablespoons lemon juice

1 teaspoon grated lemon peel

1 tablespoon capers, drained and coarsely chopped

1 red chile pepper, seeded and minced

2 tablespoons chopped chives

8 black olives, pitted and coarsely chopped

1 red onion, sliced, for garnish

Cilantro leaves, for garnish

Cut 2 wedges out of the bread and slit partially open. In a small bowl, mix the tuna and a bit of its oil with the lemon juice, lemon peel, capers, chile, chives, and olives.

Drizzle some of the remaining oil inside the bread pocket, add the tuna mixture, and garnish with the onion slices and cilantro.

Cut the mozzarella balls into thick slices and marinate them in the basil oil for 1 hour. Slice open the baguette and smear the bottom with the sun-dried tomato spread. Add the tomato and mozzarella slices, alternating between the two. Season with salt and pepper to taste and top with the basil leaves. Close the baguette and press together.

2 balls fresh mozzarella cheese

1/4 cup basil oil (page 100)

1 baguette

2 tablespoons sun-dried tomato spread (page 100)

2 ripe tomatoes, sliced

Salt

Freshly ground black pepper

12 basil leaves

Baguette *with* Mozzarella, Tomato, *and* Basil

Croissant
with Gouda, Radish,
and Walnut Spread

2 fresh croissants

2 radishes, sliced

1 tablespoon olive oil

Salt

Freshly ground black pepper

2 tablespoons walnut spread (page 102)

6 slices Gouda or Emmental cheese

1 scallion (white and green part), sliced

Red leaf lettuce

Split open the croissants. Marinate the radish slices in a mixture of the olive oil, salt, and pepper for a few minutes. Spread both croissant bottoms with the walnut spread. Layer on the cheese, radishes, scallions, and a few crisp lettuce leaves. Cover with the croissant tops.

Turkey Breast,
Fried Onions,
and White Bean Spread

1 large onion, thinly
sliced

1/4 cup olive oil

4 slices sourdough
bread

1/4 cup white bean
spread (page 99)

9 ounces turkey breast,
thinly sliced

Salt

Freshly ground black
pepper

Fry the onion slices in the olive oil over
medium heat until well browned. Spread 2
of the sourdough slices with the white bean
spread and cover with the turkey. Scatter the
browned onions over the turkey slices, season
with salt and pepper to taste, and cover with
the remaining 2 slices of bread.

Classic Hamburger
with Fried Onions

5 tablespoons olive oil

1 onion, chopped

14 ounces coarsely
ground sirloin

Salt

Freshly ground black
pepper

2 hamburger buns

mustard or
mayonnaise
(page 103)

4 tomato slices

1 red onion, cut into
rings

2 small sour pickles,
sliced

Lettuce leaves

Heat 2 tablespoons of the olive oil over
medium heat and fry the chopped onion
until golden brown. Mix the fried onions into
the ground beef, season with salt and pepper,
and form thick patties. Pour the remaining
3 tablespoons of olive oil into a nonstick pan,
bring to very high heat and fry the hamburger
patties. They should be nicely browned on
the outside and pink on the inside when
ready.

Spread the bun halves with the mustard
or mayonnaise; place the hamburger on the
bottom part and top with tomato slices, red
onion rings, sour pickles, and lettuce leaves.

Tortilla
with Smoked Salmon,
Hard-Boiled Egg,
and Avocado *Spread*

2 flour tortillas

1 cup avocado spread
(page 102)

6 slices smoked salmon

2 hard-boiled eggs,
quartered

2 scallions, trimmed
and washed

4 sprigs cilantro

Lay out the tortillas on a clean work surface. Generously smear them with the avocado spread. Layer on the smoked salmon, hard-boiled egg, scallions, and cilantro. Roll up tightly and serve.

Mediterranean Pita
with Herb Falafel

2 cups dried chickpeas

4 cups water

1 onion

4 cloves garlic

1 green chile pepper, seeded

1 cup cilantro leaves

20 mint leaves

2 teaspoons ground cumin

2 teaspoons ground coriander

1 teaspoon baking powder

Salt

Freshly ground black pepper

Olive oil for frying

Soak the chickpeas overnight in the water. Drain.

Combine the drained chickpeas with the remaining ingredients, except the oil, in a food processor and puree until it forms a coarse texture. Cover and chill for 30 minutes.

Pour oil into a heavy skillet to a height of 1 inch and heat. With moistened hands, form small, flattened balls out of the chickpea mixture and carefully lower them into the hot oil. Fry until the balls turn brown.

Serve with fresh pita bread and a variety of garnishes, such as chopped salad greens, roasted chile peppers, roasted red peppers, and grilled eggplant slices. For dressing, try: tahini, chile spread (page 102), or a yogurt sauce. Falafel is best eaten while hot.

Prosciutto,
Mozzarella,
and Artichoke Hearts

2 tablespoons olive oil

3 artichoke hearts
(frozen or canned), cut
into quarters

1 clove garlic, minced

10 black olives, pitted
and halved

Salt

Freshly ground black
pepper

4 slices walnut bread

2 tablespoons butter,
softened

3 1/2 ounces
prosciutto (Parma ham)

3 1/2 ounces
mozzarella cheese,
sliced

Heat the olive oil in a small frying pan. When hot, add the artichoke hearts and garlic and fry for 3 minutes, or until the garlic turns golden. Add the olives, season with salt and pepper to taste, and remove from heat.

Spread all 4 bread slices with butter on one side. Lay the prosciutto slices onto 2 of the buttered slices and top with the cheese. Spoon on the artichoke and olive mixture. Cover with the remaining 2 slices of bread and serve.

Shrimp, Asparagus, *and* Herb Mayonnaise

1/4 cup mayonnaise

1 teaspoon Dijon mustard

1 teaspoon lemon juice

1 clove garlic, minced

2 tablespoons minced mixed herb mixture (chives, parsley, and basil)

Salt

Freshly ground black pepper

4 slices sourdough bread

10 large shrimp, cooked and peeled

8 asparagus spears, cooked

Combine the mayonnaise, mustard, lemon juice, garlic, and herbs in a bowl. Season with salt and pepper to taste and mix well.

Spread 2 bread slices with half the mayonnaise mixture. Place the shrimp and asparagus spears on top. Dollop on the remaining mayonnaise and cover with the other 2 bread slices.

Spicy Shrimp
and Cucumber

Shrimp Marinade

1/4 cup olive oil

1 teaspoon minced
fresh ginger

2 cloves garlic, minced

1 red chile pepper,
minced

2 shallots, chopped

2 tablespoons minced
cilantro

1 teaspoon grated
lemon peel

Salt

Freshly ground black
pepper

10 large shrimp, peeled

1 tablespoon olive oil

1 tablespoon lemon
juice

Salt

Freshly ground black
pepper

1 cucumber, halved
lengthwise and cut into
4-inch strips

1 scallion, sliced into 4-
inch strips

4 slices peasant bread

Combine all the marinade ingredients in a bowl. Add the shrimp, make sure that they are well coated, and marinate for 30 minutes.

In another bowl, mix the olive oil, lemon juice, and salt and pepper to taste and add the cucumber and scallion. Let them absorb the liquid.

Heat a barbecue grill or grill pan and cook the shrimp on for 2 minutes on each side. Place the cucumber and scallion slices on 2 pieces of bread. Add the marinated shrimp and cover with the remaining bread.

BRUSCHETTA

ITALIAN

BREAD SLICES

Basic
Bruschetta

1/3 cup olive oil

2 cloves garlic, minced

2 tablespoons fresh
thyme leaves

4 slices bread (any type
is fine, sourdough is
great)

In a small mixing bowl, combine the olive
oil, garlic, and thyme leaves. Brush the
mixture onto the bread slices.

Heat up a grill pan until very hot. Place
the bread slices in the pan and grill for 3
minutes, until the bread gets blackened grill
marks and is very crispy. Turn over and do
the same for the other side.

Bruschetta is great to eat just as is or as a
base for any number of delicious toppings.

Tomato, Basil, *and* Olive

2 cloves garlic, sliced

1 green chile pepper, seeded and sliced

3 tablespoons olive oil

3 ripe tomatoes, cubed

2 scallions, chopped

10 fresh basil leaves, torn

8 black olives, pitted and sliced

Salt

Freshly ground black pepper

2 sourdough bruschetta

Fry the garlic and chile pepper in the olive oil for 2 minutes. Add the tomatoes, mix gently, and remove from heat. Add the scallions, basil, olives, and salt and pepper to taste.

Spoon the mixture over the bruschetta and serve.

Roasted Red Peppers, Anchovy, *and* Olives

4 anchovy fillets

2 bruschetta

4 roasted red pepper halves (page 98)

2 tablespoons olive oil

1 clove garlic, minced

4 black olives, pitted and sliced

6 small capers

1 tablespoon lemon juice

Salt

Freshly ground black pepper

6 sage leaves (optional)

2 to 3 tablespoons olive oil (optional)

Soak the anchovy fillets in cold water for 10 minutes in order to reduce the saltiness, then drain. On each bruschetta slice, place 2 roasted red pepper halves and 2 anchovy fillets.

Heat the olive oil in a small skillet and add the garlic, olives, and capers. Stir continuously. Add the lemon juice, bring to a boil and remove from heat. Season with salt and pepper and spoon over the peppers and anchovies.

In a small skillet, fry the sage leaves in 2 to 3 tablespoons of olive oil until crispy. Add to the bruschetta topping.

Mushrooms,
Parmesan, *and* Sage

1-ounce chunk of
Parmesan cheese

2 portobello
mushrooms

6 button mushrooms

3 tablespoons light
olive oil

2 sage leaves

1 clove garlic, minced

Salt

Freshly ground black
pepper

2 bruschetta

2 tablespoons
chopped chives

With the aid of a vegetable peeler, shave the Parmesan into thin strips. Cut the portobello mushrooms in half and then cut each half into thick slices. Cut the button mushrooms into quarters.

Heat the olive oil in a skillet and when it is very hot, add the sage, garlic, and all the mushrooms. Fry until the garlic turns golden and the mixture is well cooked, about 1 to 2 minutes. Season with salt and pepper.

Spoon the mushroom mixture onto the bruschetta and sprinkle with the chives and the Parmesan shavings.

Fried Eggplant,
Tomato, *and* Goat Cheese

2 1/3-inch-thick slices eggplant

Olive oil, for brushing

Salt

Freshly ground black pepper

2 plum tomatoes, sliced

1 teaspoon fresh thyme leaves

2 bruschetta

2 tablespoons pesto (page 98)

4 slices goat cheese

To grill the eggplant: Brush with olive oil, and season with salt and pepper. Grill for two minutes on each side or fry in a bit of olive oil in a very hot skillet till soft.

Preheat the broiler. Brush the cut side of the tomato slices with a bit of olive oil and scatter the thyme on top. Place the bruschetta on a baking sheet, spread with pesto, and then add the grilled eggplant slices, the goat cheese, and the tomatoes. Drizzle a little olive oil on top and place under the broiler for several minutes, until the cheese melts and the tomatoes begin to wilt.

Eggplant, Tomato, Chile, *and* Feta

Olive oil for frying

1 small eggplant, diced

1 clove garlic, sliced

1/2 red onion, diced

1 teaspoon fresh thyme leaves

1 green chile pepper, seeded and sliced

2 tomatoes, cubed

Salt

Freshly ground black pepper

2 bruschetta

3 1/2 ounces feta cheese, crumbled

Cilantro leaves, for garnish

Pour olive oil into a large skillet to a height of 1 inch and heat. Add the eggplant and fry until browned. Remove from the pan and drain on paper towels. Sauté the garlic, red onion, thyme, and chile pepper in a small amount of olive oil for 2 minutes. Add the tomatoes, sauté for another 2 minutes, and add the eggplant cubes. Mix well and season with salt and pepper to taste. Remove from the heat.

Place the bruschetta on a serving tray and spoon the eggplant mixture on top. Sprinkle with the crumbled feta cheese and garnish with the cilantro leaves.

Eggs Benedict
with Smoked Salmon
and Wasabi Hollandaise

2 bruschetta

4 slices smoked salmon

1 tablespoon white wine vinegar

4 eggs

1/4 cup wasabi hollandaise (page 101)

1 tablespoon chopped chives

Place the bruschetta slices on a plate and top each one with two slices of smoked salmon.

To poach the eggs: In a large, deep saucepan, pour in 2 inches of water and the white wine vinegar. Bring to a boil and lower the heat to simmer. Gently break open the eggs into the water one at a time and cook for a few minutes over a gentle boil until the whites set and the yolks are still soft. Carefully remove the eggs from the water with a slotted spoon.

For a perfect-looking egg, cut it with a cookie cutter. Place two eggs per bruschetta directly on top of the salmon and cover with the wasabi hollandaise sauce. Sprinkle with the chives. Perfect for a weekend brunch served with a chilled Bloody Mary.

Sirloin, Arugula, *and* Red Onion

1 red onion, quartered

4 to 6 tablespoons extra virgin olive oil

Coarse salt

Coarsely ground black pepper

6 thin slices of sirloin

2 fresh sage leaves, chopped

2 whole-wheat sourdough bruschetta

Fresh arugula leaves

Brush the onion quarters with a bit of the olive oil and season with salt and pepper. Marinate the sirloin slices for 1 hour in the remaining olive oil, sage, and pepper. Heat a grill pan to a very high heat; add the onion quarters and grill for about 2 minutes on each side. Set aside. Remove the sirloin from the oil mixture and grill for 1 minute over very high heat on one side only. Add the sage leaves to the pan while the sirloin is cooking.

Place the bruschetta slices on a serving plate and top each one with arugula leaves. Place three slices of sirloin on top of the arugula, sprinkle with salt, black pepper, and the sage leaves and top it off with the onion quarters.

Chicken Livers,
Onion, *and* Cherries
in Balsamic Vinegar

2 pounds fresh chicken
livers, cleaned

Salt

Freshly ground black
pepper

3 tablespoons peanut
oil or butter

1 small red onion,
thinly sliced

2 sage leaves

1 cup fresh or frozen
cherries, pitted

1 tablespoon balsamic
vinegar

2 bruschetta

Curls of 1 scallion
(page 100)

Season the chicken livers with salt and
pepper. Heat the peanut oil in a skillet and
fry the onion until golden. Add the livers and
sage and fry until browned and crisp. Add
the cherries, sauté for 1 to 2 minutes, and
season with salt and pepper. Add the balsamic
vinegar, bring to a boil, and cook for 1 minute.
Spoon the chicken livers and cherries onto
the bruschetta and scatter the scallion curls
on top.

TOASTS

EMMENTAL

Feta, Tomato, *and* Oregano

2 thick pita pockets

2 tablespoons chile spread (page 98)

5 ounces feta cheese

4 plum tomatoes, halved

Salt

Freshly ground black pepper

Olive oil

2 tablespoons fresh oregano leaves

Preheat the broiler. Split the pita pockets in half and separate. Spread 1/2 tablespoon of the chile spread on each pita half. Crumble the feta cheese on top. Top with the tomato halves, cut side up. Season with salt and pepper. Drizzle with some olive oil, sprinkle on the oregano leaves, and broil for a few minutes until the cheese melts and the tomatoes start to wilt.

Emmental,
Hard-Boiled Egg,
and Artichoke Spread

2 whole wheat rolls

2 tablespoons
artichoke heart spread
(page 103)

4 slices Emmental
cheese

2 hard-boiled eggs,
sliced

Coarse salt

Coarsely ground black
pepper

Slice open the rolls and smear the bottoms with the artichoke spread. Top with the cheese and the egg. Season with salt and pepper, cover with the roll tops, press together, and heat in a toaster oven until the cheese melts.

Mozzarella, Portobello, *and* Sage

6 tablespoons olive oil

1 clove garlic, minced

2 large portobello mushrooms

2 large balls fresh mozzarella, sliced

4 slices peasant bread

Coarse salt

Coarsely ground black pepper

4 sage leaves

Combine the olive oil and garlic in a bowl. Cut the mushrooms into thick slices and dip them in the oil and garlic mixture so that they are well coated.

Heat a grill pan to a high temperature and grill the mushrooms until browned on both sides.

Place the mozzarella on 2 bread slices. Top with the grilled mushrooms, drizzle with a little olive oil, season with salt and pepper, and top with the sage leaves. Cover with the remaining bread slices and heat in the toaster oven.

Tuna, Tomato,
and Chile Pepper

2 bagels

1 (6-ounce) can chunk light tuna, drained

2 whole canned tomatoes, drained and chopped

1 clove garlic, minced

1 green chile pepper, seeded and chopped

2 tablespoons lemon juice

1 tablespoon olive oil

Salt

Freshly ground black pepper

Slice open the bagels. Separate the tuna with a fork and mix with the remaining ingredients. Place the tuna mixture on bagel bottoms, cover with the bagel tops, and heat in the toaster oven for several minutes. Serve with green olives for a taste of the Mediterranean.

Cheddar, Feta, *and* Olives

2 1/2 ounces mild Cheddar cheese

2 1/2 ounces feta cheese

2 tablespoons olive oil

6 black or green olives, pitted and coarsely chopped

1 teaspoon oregano

Freshly ground black pepper

2 pita pockets

Coarsely grate the Cheddar cheese. Crumble up the feta cheese in a bowl and combine with the grated Cheddar. Add the olive oil, olives, and oregano, season with pepper, and mix together.

Slice open the pita pockets halfway around. Scoop the cheese mixture into the pita pockets and press down slightly. Place in toaster oven for a few minutes, until the cheese melts.

Feta, Sun-Dried Tomato, Pesto, *and* Olives

4 slices sourdough
bread

2 tablespoons pesto
(page 98)

4 slices feta cheese

2 tablespoons sun-
dried tomatoes in olive
oil, drained and
coarsely chopped

4 black olives, pitted
and halved

Spread 2 slices of the bread with the pesto.
Top with the remaining ingredients, close
the sandwich, and put in the toaster oven for
several minutes.

French Toast
with Cognac

2 eggs

1/3 cup milk

3 tablespoons heavy cream

1 tablespoon cognac

3 tablespoons butter

4 thick slices challah

In a deep bowl, beat the eggs, milk, cream, and cognac.

Heat the butter in a nonstick skillet. Dip the challah slices, one at a time, into the egg mixture until well coated on both sides. When the butter starts to sizzle add the dipped challah slices to the pan. Fry until golden and shiny on both sides.

The toast is delicious either sweet or savory and can be served with jam, honey, maple syrup, fresh fruit, crème fraîche and confectioners' sugar, or a variety of soft or hard cheeses.

Cheesy French Toast

2 pairs of challah slices (not cut all the way through)

2 eggs

1/3 cup milk

3 tablespoons heavy cream

1 tablespoon brandy

Salt

Freshly ground black pepper

4 slices Brie, Roquefort, or mozzarella cheese

3 tablespoons butter

Cut 2 slices of challah not quite to the end so that they are attached at the bottom (see photo). You'll have two pairs of challah. In a deep bowl, beat the eggs, milk, cream, and brandy. Season with salt and pepper.

Insert two slices of cheese into each challah pair and press together. Heat the butter in a nonstick skillet. Carefully dip the challah pairs into the egg mixture and when the butter starts to sizzle, place in the skillet. Fry on both sides until golden.

Open-Faced Beet
and Spicy Egg Salad

2 squares focaccia
(page 104) or 4 slices
white bread

2 tablespoons butter,
softened

2 hard-boiled eggs

1 red onion, finely
chopped

1/4 cup mayonnaise
(page 103) with a
pinch of chili powder

2 small sour pickles,
cubed

2 tablespoons
chopped fresh parsley

Salt

Freshly ground black
pepper

1 cooked beet, sliced

2 tablespoons grated
Parmesan cheese

Preheat the broiler. Slit open the focaccia
squares, creating 2 tops and 2 bottoms. Butter
the focaccia and put under the broiler for a
few seconds.

Coarsely chop the hard-boiled eggs and
mix with the onion, mayonnaise, pickles,
parsley, and salt and pepper to taste. Place
the beet slices on top of the toasted bread
slices and add a mound of the egg salad.
Sprinkle with the grated Parmesan and place
under the broiler just until it starts to brown.

Cocktail Toasts

Mini Toasts
(such as melba rounds)

Optional Toppings

Ripe figs, halved lengthwise

Goat cheese

Olive oil

Salt

Freshly ground black pepper

Dried apricots

Roquefort cheese

Walnut halves

Butter, melted

Anchovies

Tapenade (page 99)

Plum or cherry tomatoes, halved

Capers

Sage leaves

Olive Oil

Crème fraîche

Smoked salmon

Strips of lemon zest

Chives, chopped

The beauty of these cocktail toasts is that any number of ingredients can be combined for a delicious assortment. Choose among your favorites. Quantities depend on numbers of servings.

Figs: Place a fig half on each toast, cover with small piece of goat cheese, drizzle with a bit of olive oil, and season with salt and pepper. Heat under a preheated broiler until the cheese begins to melt.

Apricots: Cut a slit in each apricot and fill it with a small amount of Roquefort cheese and one walnut half. Place on the mini toast, drizzle with melted butter, and grill under a preheated broiler until the apricots start to char.

Anchovies: Place the anchovy fillets in cold water for a few minutes to reduce saltiness and then drain. Spread the mini toasts with the tapenade; layer with a tomato half, one anchovy fillet, two capers, and 1 to 2 sage leaves. Drizzle with olive oil and put under a preheated broiler for a few minutes.

Salmon: Put a dab of crème fraîche on the mini toasts. Add a small slice of smoked salmon, a strip of lemon zest, and a sprinkling of chopped chives.

SWEET SANDWICHES

Chocolate,
Raspberries,
and Orange Liqueur

2 tablespoons orange
liqueur

20 raspberries, or 10
strawberries, halved

Chocolate spread

4 slices challah

Drizzle the orange liqueur over the berries
and marinate for several minutes. Generously
spread the chocolate over the challah slices
and top with the soaked berries.

Ricotta
and Brandied Raisins

1 cup raisins

1 cup brandy or cognac

2 tablespoons sugar

1 teaspoon grated lemon peel

1 teaspoon vanilla extract

2/3 cup ricotta cheese

4 teaspoons butter, softened

Confectioners' sugar

4 slices of challah or toast

Coarsely chop the raisins and soak in a mixture of the brandy, sugar, lemon peel, and vanilla for several hours. Drain and mix the raisins with the ricotta.

Right before serving, spread one side of the bread slices with the butter and place, buttered side down, in a very hot grill pan. Remove the slices when they start to toast and show blackened grill marks. Spread 2 slices with the cheese and raisin mixture, cover with the remaining bread slices, and slightly press together. Cut in half diagonally, sprinkle with confectioners' sugar, and serve immediately. A cup of strong espresso is the perfect complement.

Peanut Butter,
Apricot, *and* Walnuts

4 dried apricots

2 tablespoons golden raisins

2 tablespoons chopped walnuts

1/4 cup peanut butter (chunky or smooth)

1/4 cup honey

4 slices raisin-walnut bread

Chop the apricots and raisins, add the walnuts, peanut butter, and honey, and mix well. Spread over 2 slices of the bread and cover with the remaining slices.

Glazed Banana,
Peanut Butter,
and Sugared Pecans

4 slices white bread

1/4 cup smooth peanut butter

4 bananas

1 teaspoon vanilla extract

2 tablespoons brown sugar

Butter for frying

2 tablespoons chopped sugared pecans

Spread the bread slices with peanut butter. Split the bananas lengthwise. Drizzle the vanilla over the cut side of the bananas and sprinkle with the brown sugar. Use the back of a spoon to press the sugar into the banana.

Heat the butter in a nonstick pan and add the bananas, cut side up. Sauté until they become golden brown. Remove from the pan and place two halves on each bread slice. Sprinkle with the sugared pecans.

Mascarpone
and Mixed Berries

2 slices challah

Butter, softened for spreading

1 cup water

4 tablespoons sugar

1 cup mixed berries (fresh or frozen)

2/3 cup mascarpone cheese

1 teaspoon grated lemon peel

Butter the bread slices.
Heat a grill pan and grill the bread slices until golden and showing blackened grill marks.

In a saucepan, combine the water and 3 tablespoons of the sugar and bring to a boil. Lower the heat and simmer for 3 minutes. Add the berries and cook for an additional minute.

Mix the mascarpone with the remaining 1 tablespoon of sugar and the lemon peel. Dollop a mound of the cheese mixture onto the bread slices and spoon on the berry mixture.

Open-Faced
Grilled Peaches

2 ripe peaches,
peeled

2 tablespoons butter,
plus extra for topping

2 tablespoons sugar

1 teaspoon grated
lemon peel

2 slices white bread

Preheat the broiler. Chop 1 peach into cubes. Sauté the peach cubes in the 2 tablespoons of butter for 5 minutes. Add 1 1/2 tablespoons of the sugar and lemon peel and continue to cook until it starts to thicken. Remove from heat, mash with a fork, and chill.

Cut the other peach into thin slices, from top to bottom. Spread the chilled peach mixture onto the 2 bread slices. Add the peach slices, cover with a bit of melted butter and sprinkle with the remaining 1/2 tablespoon of sugar. Heat under the broiler until the peaches start to brown.

Ricotta *and* Grilled Apricots

1 cup water

1 cup sugar, plus extra for topping

Zest of 1 lemon

1 vanilla bean, split open lengthwise

6 fresh apricots, halved

Butter, softened for spreading

2 slices sourdough bread or challah

1 cup ricotta cheese

Preheat the broiler. In a small saucepan over medium heat, combine the water, sugar, lemon zest, and vanilla bean halves. Bring to a boil and cook for 10 minutes. Add the apricots, lower the heat, and cook for 5 additional minutes. Turn off the heat and let the apricots cool in the syrup for several minutes.

Butter the bread slices and place under the broiler until toasted. Remove the slices and generously spread them with the ricotta cheese. Top with the cooked apricot halves, drizzle with the apricot syrup, and sprinkle with sugar. Heat for a few minutes under the broiler.

Baked Figs
and Almond Cream

8 slices challah

8 ripe figs

2 tablespoons butter, softened

2 tablespoons sugar

Almond Cream

3 tablespoons crushed almonds

1/4 cup sugar

2 eggs

1 cup milk

1 cup heavy cream

1 teaspoon vanilla extract

Preheat the oven to 350° F.

To prepare the almond cream, combine all the ingredients and mix well.

Cut the bread slices on the diagonal to form triangles. Slice each fig in half lengthwise. Grease an 8 by 10-inch baking pan with the butter. Layer the bread triangles alternately with the fig slices (see photo). Pour the almond cream over it and sprinkle with the sugar. Bake for 15 to 20 minutes.

Wonderful served alone or with vanilla ice cream.

BETWEEN
the BREAD

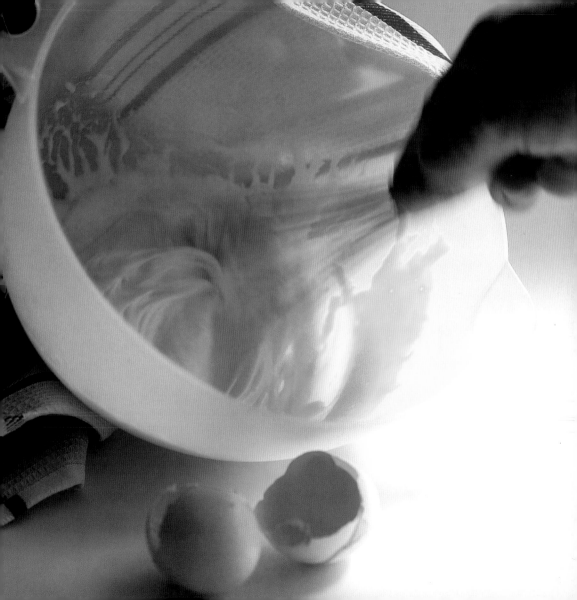

Marinated Roasted Peppers

4 red bell peppers or chile peppers

1/4 cup olive oil

1 clove garlic, thinly sliced

1 teaspoon fresh thyme leaves

Singe the peppers over a burner with a high flame, turning frequently, until the skin is blackened and starts to blister. Remove from the flame, let cool. In a shallow dish, mix together the olive oil, garlic, and thyme. Peel away the skins from the peppers and discard the stems and seeds. Cut the peppers into halves or strips and add to the marinade, turning to coat completely.

Chile Spread

5 red chile peppers, seeded

2 cloves garlic

1-inch piece of fresh ginger, peeled

2 shallots

1 cup cilantro leaves

1 teaspoon cumin seeds

Salt

Freshly ground black pepper

1 cup olive oil

Place all the ingredients in food processor and process until it forms a grainy texture. Store chilled in a glass jar or airtight container.

Pesto

1 cup fresh basil leaves

2 cloves garlic

3 tablespoons pine nuts

3 tablespoons grated Parmesan cheese

Salt

Freshly ground black pepper

1/2 cup olive oil

In a food processor, combine the basil, garlic, pine nuts, Parmesan, and salt and pepper to taste. Gradually add in the olive oil and puree until the mixture becomes green and smooth.

White Bean Spread

2 cups white beans (such as kidney or navy beans)

4 cups cold water

1 onion, peeled and quartered

4 sprigs thyme

1 sprig rosemary

3 cloves garlic

1/3 cup olive oil

Salt

Freshly ground black pepper

Place the beans in the cold water and soak overnight. Drain, put into a saucepan along with the onion, thyme, rosemary, and garlic. Cover with water, bring to a boil, then lower the heat and cook for 2 hours, or until the beans are soft. Drain.

Puree the beans in a food processor, gradually adding in the olive oil. Season with salt and pepper to taste. The mixture should be creamy in texture.

Tapenade

1 cup good-quality black olives, pitted

2 cloves garlic

1 tablespoon fresh thyme leaves

Freshly ground black pepper

1/4 cup light olive oil

In a food processor, combine the olives, garlic, thyme, and black pepper and puree. Gradually add the olive oil and continue to puree until the mixture is black and smooth.

Sun-Dried Tomato Spread

1 cup sun-dried tomatoes

2 cloves garlic

1 teaspoon fresh thyme leaves

1 dried red chile pepper

1/3 cup olive oil

Put all the ingredients in a food processor and process until it forms a slightly grainy texture. Store chilled in an airtight container.

Basil Oil

2 cups water

1 cup basil leaves

1 1/4 cups light olive oil

Boil the water and blanch the basil leaves for a few seconds. Drain the leaves, dry them, and combine with the oil in a food processor. Puree until the mixture becomes smooth.

Let the mixture stand for several hours. Strain the oil (it should be clear and green in color) and store in a glass jar or airtight container.

Scallion Curls

3 very fresh scallions

Cold water

Ice cubes

Clean the scallions and cut into 4-inch-long pieces. (Use the white part as well as the green.) Slice each piece lengthwise into very thin strips and place in a bowl with the cold water and ice cubes. After 15 minutes they should be curled. Use as a garnish.

Balsamic Roasted Onions and Garlic

5 small red onions, halved or thinly sliced

20 cloves garlic

3 tablespoons balsamic vinegar

3 tablespoons olive oil

2 tablespoons sugar

Preheat the oven to 325°F. Place the onions in a baking pan. If using onion halves, place them cut side up and slightly separate the layers from each other. Add the garlic and drizzle with the balsamic vinegar and olive oil. Make sure that the liquids seep in between the layers of the onion halves. Sprinkle with the sugar, cover with aluminum foil, and bake for 30 minutes. Remove the aluminum foil and continue to bake for another 30 minutes.

Hollandaise Sauce

2 egg yolks

1/4 cup butter, melted

2 tablespoons lemon juice

Salt

Freshly ground black pepper

In a small mixing bowl or saucepan, whisk the egg yolks. Rest the bowl over a pot of simmering water and continue to whisk over the steaming water for 2 minutes. Add the melted butter in a thin stream and continue to whisk until the mixture becomes smooth, velvety, and thick. Add the lemon juice and season with salt and pepper.

Variation: Add 1 teaspoon of wasabi powder at the end if you want wasabi hollandaise.

Walnut Spread

1 1/2 cups walnuts
1 clove garlic
1/3 cup light olive oil
Pinch of nutmeg

Salt
Freshly ground black pepper

In a food processor, coarsely grind the walnuts and garlic. Gradually add in the olive oil while continuing to run the motor until the mixture forms a paste. Add the nutmeg and salt and pepper to taste. Store in the refrigerator.

Avocado Spread

2 ripe avocados
1 red onion, finely chopped
3 tablespoons olive oil
1/4 cup freshly squeezed lemon juice
1 green chile pepper, seeded and minced

Salt
Freshly ground black pepper

Mash the avocados in a bowl. Add the onion, olive oil, lemon juice, and chile pepper and mix well. Season with salt and pepper and store in the refrigerator.

Artichoke Heart Spread

6 frozen artichoke
hearts, sliced

1/4 cup olive oil

2 cloves garlic,
smashed

1/2 onion, finely
chopped

1 teaspoon fresh
thyme leaves

1 tablespoon pine
nuts

Salt

Freshly ground black
pepper

In a skillet over medium heat, fry the artichoke slices in the olive oil for about 2 minutes. Add the garlic, onion, and thyme, lower the heat and sauté for several minutes, until the artichokes soften. Pour the mixture into a food processor and puree. Add the pine nuts and continue to puree. Season with salt and pepper to taste and store in a glass jar or airtight container in the refrigerator.

Mayonnaise

3 egg yolks

1/2 cup olive oil

1/2 cup corn oil

2 tablespoons lemon
juice

1 tablespoon Dijon
mustard

Salt

Freshly ground black
pepper

In a mixing bowl, beat the egg yolks for 1 minute. Whisk in the olive oil and corn oil in a thin stream—make sure that you add them very gradually and in small amounts. The mixture will start to emulsify. Add the lemon juice, mustard, and salt and pepper to taste.

For flavored mayonnaise add any of the following: 2 to 3 garlic cloves, minced (for aioli); mixed herbs (mince 1 tablespoon parsley, 1 tablespoon chives, and 1/2 tablespoon mint leaves); 1 to 2 tablespoons wasabi powder or 1 tablespoon of harissa (a hot sauce in Middle Eastern markets).

Focaccia

1 ounce fresh yeast

3 tablespoons sugar

3 cups water

1 tablespoon salt

1/4 cup olive oil, plus extra for sprinkling

1 tablespoon fresh rosemary leaves, chopped

5 1/4 cups all-purpose flour

Coarse salt, for sprinkling on top of dough

Put the yeast, 1 tablespoon of the sugar, and 1 cup of the water in a mixing bowl and stir well. Set aside for 30 minutes. Add the remaining 2 tablespoons sugar and 2 cups water and the salt, olive oil, rosemary, and flour to the yeast mixture and, using an electric mixer fitted with a dough hook, mix for 5 minutes. Don't worry if the dough is very soft, it should be. Place the dough in the oven on a baking sheet (the oven should *not* be on), cover with a clean, damp kitchen towel and allow it to rise for an hour.

Using oiled hands, flatten out the dough on a large baking sheet to a uniform thickness and let rest for another 30 minutes. Preheat the oven to 425°F. Using your fingertips, press down on the dough and make small dimples. Sprinkle with a little olive oil and coarse salt. Bake for 20 minutes or until it browns and your kitchen is filled with the most wonderful smell.